Good Morning, Monster Town

PHASE 5

/a_e/
o_e/

Level 8 – Purple

Helpful Hints for Reading at Home

The graphemes (written letters) and phonemes (units of sound) used throughout this series are aligned with Letters and Sounds. This offers a consistent approach to learning whether reading at home or in the classroom.

HERE IS A LIST OF PHONEMES FOR THIS PHASE OF LEARNING. AN EXAMPLE OF THE PRONUNCIATION CAN BE FOUND IN BRACKETS.

Phase 5			
ay (day)	ou (out)	ie (tie)	ea (eat)
oy (boy)	ir (girl)	ue (blue)	aw (saw)
wh (when)	ph (photo)	ew (new)	oe (toe)
au (Paul)	a_e (make)	e_e (these)	i_e (like)
o_e (home)	u_e (rule)		

Phase 5 Alternative Pronunciations of Graphemes			
a (hat, what)	e (bed, she)	i (fin, find)	o (hot, so, other)
u (but, unit)	c (cat, cent)	g (got, giant)	ow (cow, blow)
ie (tied, field)	ea (eat, bread)	er (farmer, herb)	ch (chin, school, chef)
y (yes, by, very)	ou (out, shoulder, could, you)		

HERE ARE SOME WORDS WHICH YOUR CHILD MAY FIND TRICKY.

Phase 5 Tricky Words			
oh	their	people	Mr
Mrs	looked	called	asked
could			

TOP TIPS FOR HELPING YOUR CHILD TO READ:

• Allow children time to break down unfamiliar words into units of sound and then encourage children to string these sounds together to create the word.

• Encourage your child to point out any focus phonics when they are used.

• Read through the book more than once to grow confidence.

• Ask simple questions about the text to assess understanding.

• Encourage children to use illustrations as prompts.

PHASE 5
/a_e/
/o_e/

This book focuses on the phonemes /a_e/ and /o_e/ and is a purple level 8 book band.

Good Morning, Monster Town

Written by
John Wood

Illustrated by
Kris Jones

It was a cold winter's night in Monster Town. All the monsters were sleeping. All was quiet, apart from the wind and the snores of the oldest monsters.

Most of the monsters were having nightmares. They were dreaming about a very scary monster. The monster they dreamed of made all the children and grown-up monsters shake with fear.

The monster's name was Grome. He lived in a cave on the hill. It was his job to wake all the monsters up in the morning so the grown-ups could go to work and the children could go to their classes.

As the Sun rose, Grome grabbed his trombone. He blew hard. The blare of the trombone made the houses quake and the trees tremble.

Grome played one more low note just to make sure the last few monsters were awake. BRRRUMP, went the trombone.

As soon as the sound of the trombone had faded, the town began to stir. All of a sudden, there were monsters all over town. The monsters were cross and annoyed as they got ready for the day ahead.

High on the hill, Grome sat with Jane. Jane was a talking bird, but she didn't say much. "It's not fair," said Grome, his voice sad as he spoke.

"I need to wake them up, or they will be late," said Grome. "But they all hate me."
Jane was about to speak, but instead she patted her friend's head.

Down in the town, three monsters were walking to their classes.
"I hate that trombone," said the fat monster.
"Me too," said the thin monster.

The long monster had an idea. She poked the other monsters and whispered something. "I have a plan for tomorrow," she said. Then she tapped her nose. That meant it was a secret.

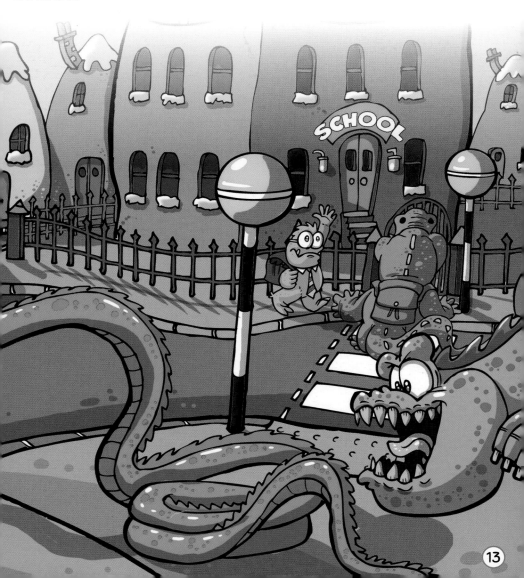

The next morning, Grome was getting ready to wake the monsters up. Just before the Sun rose, he opened his trombone case, then gasped in shock.

Someone had stolen his trombone! Grome didn't know what to do. He had to wake the monsters up or they'd all be late!

Grome ran outside to shake his maracas. The maracas were too quiet. He sang at the same time. But Grome's voice didn't make much noise.

Grome dropped his maracas. All those years of maraca practice had been a complete waste. "I'm going to need the big maracas," said Grome. He ran back into his cave.

But Grome couldn't find the big maracas. Instead, he grabbed his vibraphone and two sticks. "I hope this will work," he said. He was running out of ideas.

But the vibraphone had a calm and peaceful sound. Grome felt tired. Luckily, one of the sticks broke and hit him in the face. That woke him up!

Grome went back inside and got the biggest tuba he could find. He dragged it out of the cave and blew it as hard as he could.

But no sound came out of the hole. Grome looked closer. The tuba was full of mud and a tired mole.

"Oh no," said Grome. "The monsters will be late!"

Then Jane flew past. "Jane!" said Grome. "I'm glad you are here. Can you ask the other birds to help me wake all the monsters up? Please?" Jane nodded and flew away again.

Soon the sound of birdsong drifted down to
Monster Town. The sound was fantastic. One
by one, the monsters woke up. It was the
perfect way to start the day.

The little monsters went to their classes and the big monsters went to work. They were smiling and waving.

"You must ask the birds to help you all the time!" one monster suggested to Grome as she rode to work on her bike.
"That is a great idea! I'll ask them right away," said Grome as he waved back.

The next morning, the monsters were dozing in their homes. All of a sudden, there was a horrid sound. Whatever was making the sound was getting closer and closer.

The monsters rose from their beds. They covered their ears with their hands. They stuffed their faces into pillows. The sound was getting louder and louder and LOUDER.

It was a giant flock of birds, and each one of them was playing a little trombone! The big brass band of birds swept along the streets. Windows were smashed. Trombones squawked. The town was full of fanfare and feathers.

"This is not what we meant at all!" the monsters shouted. But no one could hear a thing over the sound of trombones.

Good Morning, Monster Town

1.   What were the monsters dreaming about?

2.   Why does Grome think everyone hates him?

3.   What was stolen from Grome?

4.   What sort of animal is Jane?

   (a)   A bird

   (b)   A monkey

   (c)   A snake

5.   How do you think the monsters felt when the giant flock of birds arrived? Do you think the birds were helpful?

©This edition published 2021.
First published in 2020.
BookLife Publishing Ltd.
King's Lynn, Norfolk PE30 4LS

ISBN 978-1-83927-315-5

Good Morning, Monster Town
Written by John Wood
Illustrated by Kris Jones

An Introduction to BookLife Readers...

Our Readers have been specifically created in line with the London Institute of Education's approach to book banding and are phonetically decodable and ordered to support each phase of the Letters and Sounds document.

Each book has been created to provide the best possible reading and learning experience. Our aim is to share our love of books with children, providing both emerging readers and prolific page-turners with beautiful books that are guaranteed to provoke interest and learning, regardless of ability.

BOOK BAND GRADED using the Institute of Education's approach to levelling.

PHONETICALLY DECODABLE supporting each phase of Letters and Sounds.

EXERCISES AND QUESTIONS to offer reinforcement and to ascertain comprehension.

BEAUTIFULLY ILLUSTRATED to inspire and provoke engagement, providing a variety of styles for the reader to enjoy whilst reading through the series.

AUTHOR INSIGHT:
JOHN WOOD

An incredibly creative and talented author, John Wood has written about 60 books for BookLife Publishing. Born in Warwickshire, he graduated with a BA in English Literature and English Language from De Montfort University. During his studies, he learned about literature, styles of language, linguistic relativism, and psycholinguistics, which is the study of the effects of language on the brain. Thanks to his learnings, John successfully uses words that captivate and resonate with children and that will be sure to make them retain information. His stories are entertaining, memorable, and extremely fun to read.

PHASE 5
/a_e/
o_e/

This book focuses on the phonemes /a_e/ and /o_e/ and is a purple level 8 book band.